OUTLAW IN TROUBLE

Jasmine turned back to Outlaw. "We've got lots of work to do," she said to him. "We have to review cantering."

Outlaw raised his head. He looked at Jasmine as if she were totally nuts. He snorted. He reared, jerking the lead rope out of Jasmine's hand, and took off.

Jasmine took off after him, but Outlaw was fast.

"Outlaw!" Jasmine yelled, still running. "Don't run! You could hurt yourself."

Outlaw put his head down and ran as fast as he could.

"Please," Jasmine called. "I'll never mention the show again."

Outlaw stumbled and fell.

Jasmine's First
Horse Show

BONNIE BRYANT

Illustrated by Marcy Ramsey

A SKYLARK BOOK
NEW YORK • TORONTO • LONDON • SYDNEY • AUCKLAND

RL 3, 007–010
JASMINE'S FIRST HORSE SHOW
A Bantam Skylark Book / August 1997

*Skylark Books is a registered trademark of Bantam Books,
a division of Bantam Doubleday Dell Publishing Group, Inc.
Registered in U.S. Patent and Trademark Office and elsewhere.
Pony Tails is a registered trademark of Bonnie Bryant Hiller.
"USPC" and "Pony Club" are registered trademarks of The
United States Pony Clubs, Inc., The Kentucky Horse Park,
4071 Iron Works Pike, Lexington, KY 40511-8462.*

ISBN 0-553-48483-4

Published simultaneously in the United States and Canada.

*Bantam Books are published by Bantam Books, a division of Bantam
Doubleday Dell Publishing Group, Inc. Its trademark, consisting of the
words "Bantam Books" and the portrayal of a rooster, is Registered
in U.S. Patent and Trademark Office and in other countries. Marca
Registrada. Bantam Books, 1540 Broadway, New York, New York
10036.*

PRINTED IN THE UNITED STATES OF AMERICA

OPM   0   9   8   7   6   5   4   3   2   1

*I would like to give my special thanks
to Helen Geraghty for her help
in the writing of this book.*

Hi, we're the **PONY TAILS**—May Grover, Corey Takamura, and Jasmine James. We're neighbors, we're best friends, and most of all, we're pony-crazy.

My name is **May.** My pony is named Macaroni after my favorite food, macaroni and cheese. He's the sweetest pony in the world! Jasmine and Corey say he's the exact opposite of me. Of course, they're just teasing. I have two older sisters who say I'm a one-girl disaster area, but they're not teasing. Would you like some used sisters? I have two for sale.

I'm called **Corey**—short for Corinne. I live between Jasmine and May—in a lot of ways. My house is between theirs. I'm between them in personality, too. Jasmine's organized, May's forgetful, and I can be both. May's impulsive, Jasmine's cautious, and I'm just reasonable. My pony is named Samurai. He's got a white blaze on his face shaped like a samurai sword. Sam is temperamental, but he's mine and I love him.

I'm **Jasmine.** My pony is named Outlaw. His face is white, like an outlaw's mask. He can be as unpredictable as an outlaw, too, but I'd never let him go to jail because I love him to pieces! I like to ride him, and I also like to look after him. I have a baby sister named Sophie. When she gets older I'm going to teach her to ride.

So why don't you tack up and have fun with us on our pony adventures!

May Corey Jasmine

JASMINE'S HOUSE

COREY'S HOUSE

MAY'S HOUSE

Jasmine's First
Horse Show

1 Jitters

Jasmine was embarrassed to read what she'd just written. But Corey and May were her best friends, and she had to be honest. "Here goes," she said with a groan. She picked up the sheet of paper that was marked "Equitation Class." Max Regnery of Pine Hollow Stables had asked all riders in the upcoming horse show to write down their goals for each class. The three friends were in Jasmine's room discussing what they had written.

" 'In Equitation I want to keep my wrists relaxed, my knees in, my heels down, my posture straight,' " she read.

"That's it?" asked May with a grin.

Jasmine felt herself turn from pink to red. "There's more. 'I want to make sure I don't post too high on the trot.' " In posting, riders move up and down in the saddle. A rider who rises too high can lose control and wind up bouncing. That was *truly* bad form. " 'I want my seat in the canter to be smooth, just an inch or two out of the saddle.' "

"It's your first horse show!" said Corey. "You can't be perfect. Nobody is ever perfect, not even great riders."

May crossed her arms. "I have a mission for you."

Jasmine groaned. Another goal!

"I want you to throw away that list," May said. "And I want you to come up with one single goal for Equitation."

Jasmine's heart sank. If she only had one goal and she missed that goal, she would be miserable. But she knew May and Corey were right. She closed her eyes, trying to think of the right goal. She found it and opened her eyes again. "I don't want to make a complete idiot of myself."

"Put it positively," Corey said. Max had

told them all their goals had to be about hopes, not fears.

"I want to be"—Jasmine took a deep breath—"poised." It sounded so stupid. It was like wanting to be beautiful, or a genius.

"Good goal," May said. "Write it down, put it in the envelope, and seal the envelope so you can't change your mind."

As Jasmine licked the envelope, her heart fluttered. Now she couldn't take it back.

"What about your goals for Showing and Sitting and the Pony Pleasure Class?" asked Corey.

Jasmine grinned. Those were easy. "I want to look relaxed even if I'm not. I want Outlaw to hold his head proudly. Of course, that means I have to give him something to be proud of. I want him to show his natural talent."

May nodded. "And what about the Relay Race?"

Jasmine had been thinking about the Relay Race for weeks. She had been imagining that she might save the day, bringing her team from far, far behind.

3

She was ashamed to tell Corey and May that she had imagined the crowd on its feet cheering as she crossed the finish line.

May must have had some idea what Jasmine was thinking because she nodded and said, "Don't worry. The important thing is to have a goal."

Jasmine pulled a slip from another envelope. " 'My goal for the Relay Race is not to drop the egg and have it splatter all over the ring the way it did at the last practice,' " she read.

"Outstanding," said May and Corey together.

"Max will like that one," said May.

"Not after I screw up," Jasmine said. She licked the envelope and sealed it. Now her goals were set.

"My goals are pretty humdrum," Corey said. "I want to keep Samurai interested during Showing and Sitting and Pleasure Class." Sam got bored easily and showed it, which judges did not like. "I want to keep my heels down and my wrists relaxed in the Pony Hunter Class." This class was judged on style, rather than

4

speed, so a rider's form was very important.

May read her goals. " 'In the first two
classes I want to be calm. Sometimes I get
so excited I make Macaroni nervous. In
the Pony Hunter Class I want to take my
time and not rush. In the Relay Race I
want to get the team keyed up without
turning them into nervous wrecks.' " May
groaned. "In other words, I don't want to
be me. I want to be some nice, cool, calm,
collected person."

"Hey," said Corey with a grin. "You
never know."

The girls sealed their envelopes. They
had to give them to Max at the beginning
of the horse show. He would use them in
judging Best in Show.

"We could win all the events," Corey
said dreamily.

May got a faraway look in her eyes. "If
we sweep all the events, we'll be . . ."

"The Dream Team," Corey and May
said together. They gave each other high
fives. They were about to say "Jake,"
which was what the Pony Tails did when
they said the same thing at the same time.

5

But Corey and May realized that Jasmine had fallen silent.

They looked at her.

"I'm not dream material," Jasmine said. "It's my first show."

"You're a natural," said Corey with a grin. "Say it. Dream Team."

"Dream Team," Jasmine said softly.

"Louder," said May.

"Dream Team," Jasmine said as May and Corey joined in. They gave each other a Pony Tail super high five, which was actually a high ten because they used both hands. Then they said, "Jake."

The Pony Tails weren't a club. They were best friends, which was even better.

"We should have badges or something so everyone will know we're the Dream Team," said Corey.

"Max wants all riders to be Pine Hollow riders and nothing else," May explained. "So we can't wear badges."

"I can see that," Corey said, "but could we have a secret sign? Something that only we recognize?"

"I'm getting an idea," May said. She raised a finger.

7

Corey and Jasmine looked at each other and grinned. May's great ideas were something else.

"We're the Pony Tails, right?" said May.

The other two nodded.

"So we'll wear ponytails," said May triumphantly.

Corey and May heaved sighs of relief. For once May's great idea *was* great.

"No one will know but us," May said. But then she jumped up and looked at her watch. "I promised my mother I'd clean my closet this afternoon."

"That's a first," Corey said, standing up.

"No clean closet, no horse show," said May. She dashed out the door.

"I told my mother I'd see how Gorilla is doing," Corey said.

"Gorilla?" Jasmine asked. Corey's mother, Dr. Takamura, was a veterinarian. Doc Tock, as everyone called her, took care of strange animals from time to time, but a gorilla? "Where do you keep a gorilla? I know you have a big stable, but gorillas need a lot of room."

"Actually, Gorilla is a kitten," Corey said with a grin. "He's really bossy. So we call him Gorilla. Want to meet him?"

Usually Jasmine would have loved to meet a cat that acted like a gorilla, but she couldn't get her mind off the show.

"Later," she said.

"I'll tell Gorilla you said hello," Corey said, taking off and leaving Jasmine alone in her room.

Jasmine wandered over to her desk and picked up the riding book the riders at Pine Hollow used. She opened it to the section on equitation.

Jasmine was good at equitation. She always kept her heels down and her knees in. But you can never be too well prepared, she thought. She opened the book to a page headed "The Correct Seat." It showed examples of stirrups too long and stirrups too short, and of a rider with a back too round and a back too stiff. And then it showed a picture of a rider with a perfect seat.

Jasmine thought maybe she should go out and get on Outlaw to check her seat. But she wasn't allowed to ride alone, and

May and Corey were busy. So what could she do?

Jasmine loved to draw. One of the ways she got better at riding was by drawing ponies and riders. She realized that drawing would be a good way of getting ready for the show, and it would be fun, too. She picked up her drawing pad.

But the pony she drew had a huge head and a tiny tail. And the rider looked as if she was about to fall off. Jasmine crumpled the drawing and tossed it at the wastebasket.

She missed.

"Some great athlete I am," she muttered. "I'll probably fall right out of the saddle."

She drew another horse. This one looked more like a pig than a pony.

"Forget it," she said. She crumpled up the sheet of paper and tossed it at the wastebasket.

The paper flew past the wastebasket and out the door of her room.

"What's this?" said her father's voice. He stuck his head into her room.

"I can't even hit the wastebasket," she said. "I'm hopeless."

Her father smoothed out the sheet of paper. He didn't say anything, but Jasmine saw him blink with surprise.

"It's the worst drawing ever," she said.

He put his arm around her. "What's up, Jazzie?"

Jasmine liked it when he called her that. "Corey and May have been in pony shows before, so it's no big deal for them. But I've never been in a show before, and"—she took a deep breath—"I'm going to make a total fool of myself."

Mr. James smoothed her hair. "You'll be great. The thing is not to try too hard." He sat on the window seat beside her. "When I'm working on an experiment, sometimes I want it to work so much that I try too hard." Mr. James was an ecologist. "When I do that I ruin it."

"That's me," Jasmine said. "I'm going to wreck everything."

"You have to let things take their course," Mr. James said. "You have to let serendipity happen."

Jasmine giggled. Her dad was a profes-

11

sor of ecology, and he was always using five-dollar words. "What's serendipity?" she asked.

Her father grinned. "Luck."

"I don't feel lucky," Jasmine said gloomily.

Her father hugged her. "Wait and see."

2 Out of the Gloom

May opened her eyes. Something was wrong. Plunk, her cat, was on the dresser, ears perked, tail straight up. He was worried.

May sat straight up. It was still dark, but Plunk seemed to be watching something. May got out of bed. The floor was cold under her bare feet. She crossed her arms, trying to warm herself, and tiptoed toward the window. She peered outside and thought she saw someone moving across the Jameses' yard. It was Jasmine.

"I don't believe it," May muttered. She pulled on her jeans, a T-shirt, and a sweatshirt. She padded down to the mud-

13

room and pulled on her rubber boots because she knew the grass would be covered with dew.

Yawning, May walked out of her house. Next to her yard was Corey's yard. Beyond it was Jasmine's yard. And there was Jasmine feeding Outlaw a carrot while she talked to him.

May shook her head. The horse show wasn't until Saturday, five days away, and already Jasmine was lecturing Outlaw. What had happened to Jasmine's goal of letting Outlaw shine on his own?

May walked onto the Pony Trail, the path that linked the Pony Tails' three backyards. She was planning to point out to Jasmine that six in the morning was too early to achieve perfection. But as May got closer, she could see that Jasmine had put her arms around Outlaw's neck as if she were hanging on to him for dear life.

"Hi," May said.

Jasmine jumped. "Hi," she said, brushing her hair out of her eyes. "Don't you love early mornings?"

May was about to say that she loved to

14

get up at the crack of dawn. But she was afraid Jasmine might take her seriously. "I'm hungry," May said. "I woke up thinking about food. You know me, I hate to eat alone, so I came looking to see if I could find someone to eat with me."

"For real?" Jasmine asked.

"Can't you hear my stomach growling?" May asked.

Jasmine listened, but she couldn't hear May's stomach growling. Still, it was nice to have company, so she said, "I could eat."

She and May walked Outlaw to the pasture behind the barn. Then they headed for May's house.

"How come you're up so early?" May asked.

"I was riding in my dreams. And everything I did was wrong," Jasmine said. "My heels were up and my wrists were down and the reins kept slipping through my fingers."

May knew Jasmine needed to think about something else. So she said, "I've got this great idea for a super-duper cereal. I'm thinking about packaging it,

16

selling it nationwide, and becoming a millionaire." The idea had only occurred to May that minute. But already it sounded good.

"Only a millionaire?" asked Jasmine with a grin. "What's wrong with being a billionaire?"

"I'm saving that for my teens," May said.

"What's up?" said a voice over their heads. They looked up and saw Corey peering out of her bedroom window.

"You're in luck," May said. "You're about to have the greatest breakfast experience of your life."

"I can't wait," Corey said. Her head disappeared from the window, and she was downstairs in minutes.

Soon Corey and Jasmine were sitting at the table in May's kitchen. May was standing at the counter preparing breakfast. She poured puffed rice into a big bowl. She tossed raisins on top and sprinkled walnuts and sunflower seeds on top of them. Then she scattered some coconut over all that. To top it off, she lobbed in a handful of chocolate chips.

17

May filled three smaller bowls and carried them to the table. "Dig in," she said.

Corey took the first spoonful. She chewed. Her eyes widened. She swallowed. "It's good, but I could do without the coconut."

"And the sunflower seeds are a little too much," said Jasmine with a grin.

"And the chocolate chips are over the top," said Corey.

"And the walnuts and raisins don't add much," said Jasmine.

"But the puffed rice is good," Corey said. "I think you've got something, May. Puffed rice for breakfast."

May groaned.

"What's this?" said Mrs. Grover, who was standing in the doorway.

"Great cereal," May said.

"Then why is there coconut in the soap dish?" asked Mrs. Grover, holding up a sliver of coconut.

"A mere accident," May said. "Part of the creative process."

"And sunflower seeds in the cat bowl?" asked Mrs. Grover.

"I guess I got a little sloppy," May said.

"If you want to be in the horse show, May, you are going to have to clean this up," Mrs. Grover said.

"Ho boy," May said.

There were nuts on the kitchen sponge and a curl of coconut next to the telephone.

"As a slob I have talent," May said. "I wonder if this could lead to a career."

"Look at this," Corey said. She lifted a chocolate chip out of the juicer. "Chocolate orange juice could be great."

"Hey, what about chocolate carrot juice?" May said.

As they rinsed out the juicer, Corey said, "How come it's so easy to make a mess, and so hard to clean up?"

"That's one of life's mysteries," said May.

They put the juicer back on the counter and swept the floor and loaded the dishwasher. "Next time I have a great idea, stop me," said May.

"Are we done?" Jasmine asked. She glanced toward the door, clearly wanting

19

to be on her way. Corey and May looked at her in surprise. It wasn't like Jasmine to rush off.

"What's up?" Corey said.

"Nothing much," Jasmine said. "A few odds and ends. See you, guys." She headed for the door and left.

"What's with her?" asked Corey.

"I found her talking to Outlaw this morning. She was giving him show tips," May said.

"She's got to relax," Corey said.

"But the more you tell her to relax, the more nervous she gets," said May.

They went to look for Jasmine.

Jasmine was in the pasture with Outlaw. He was trying to munch on tender green grass while Jasmine gave him instructions. "You have a nice long stride," she said to him. "Don't lose it under pressure." Outlaw shook his head. His white mask stood out against his dark chestnut coat. He looked frazzled.

May and Corey looked at each other. Pretty soon Outlaw was going to be a nervous wreck.

"We're going over to Pine Hollow,"

Corey said. "Max wants every saddle cleaned before the show on Saturday. Why don't you come?"

"Maybe later," Jasmine said.

"I was thinking we could have a picnic at the PTSP," Corey said. There was a special spot on the hill behind Pine Hollow that the Pony Tails called the PTSP, the Pony Tails' Special Place. They were convinced that sandwiches tasted better there.

"I think I'd better stay here," Jasmine said.

Corey and May looked at each other. If they kept bugging Jasmine, she'd get even more nervous.

"See you," Corey said.

"Take care," said May.

3 Outlaw in Trouble

"I hate to see Jasmine so worried," May said.

"I guess it's something she has to get through," Corey said. But she knew what May meant. Usually the Pony Tails were the world's greatest threesome. Now they weren't. Jasmine seemed to be in her own world.

"I could use a ride," Corey said. When the Pony Tails were upset, a ride could usually cheer them up. But they were on their way to Pine Hollow Stables, and that was too far for them to ride alone.

May's father came whistling out of the Grovers' barn. He was a horse trainer, so he worked at home.

"Hi, girls," he said. He took another look at them. "Is something wrong?"

"Jasmine has horse show nerves," May said.

Mr. Grover looked over to where Jasmine was talking earnestly to Outlaw. "I remember my first horse show," he said. "I kept wishing I would break my arm so I wouldn't have to ride."

May blinked in surprise. "You?"

Mr. Grover nodded. "It's one of the worst memories I have."

"*I* hoped there would be an earthquake so my first horse show would be canceled," Corey said.

"Some people hope for lightning and thunder," Mr. Grover said. "Or an invasion of ants. It depends."

May and Corey exchanged grins. Mr. Grover always knew how to make them feel better.

"How come you guys aren't on horseback?" Mr. Grover said. "It's a perfect day for riding."

"We're going to Pine Hollow Stables, and it's too far to ride alone," said May.

"Hmmm," said Mr. Grover, rubbing

23

his chin. "I might have the solution to that problem. I have to talk to Max and his mother about something. Why don't the three of us saddle up and ride over?"

"I could handle that," May said. She hugged him. "You are the world's greatest father."

Corey sighed. Looking at May and her father with their arms around each other made her miss her own father. Corey's parents were divorced. She saw her father a lot, and she loved him as much as ever, but it wasn't the same as when he lived with her and her mother.

May must have known what Corey was feeling because she swept her into the hug. Corey felt a lot better. She reminded herself of what she'd told Jasmine: Nothing is ever perfect.

"So let's ride," said May happily. The girls went to get Samurai and Macaroni.

A few minutes later Corey rode Sam over to the Grovers' barn, where May and her father were waiting.

"Tallyho!" said May. "Let's go."

As they rode into the pasture behind

the barns, they saw Jasmine and Outlaw. She had her arms around his neck, and she was talking a mile a minute. Outlaw looked miserable.

"You're sure you don't want to come?" May called to Jasmine. "My father's with us, so we can ride to Pine Hollow."

Jasmine shook her head. She watched Corey and May and Mr. Grover ride to the top of the hill. The ground was boggy after a recent rain, so they went slowly. At the top of the hill they turned to wave. Macaroni's yellow mane blew back in the wind. The blaze like a curved sword on Samurai's nose shone in the morning light. Then they disappeared on the far side of the hill.

Jasmine turned back to Outlaw. "We've got lots of work to do," she said to him. "We have to review cantering."

Outlaw raised his head. He looked at Jasmine as if she were totally nuts. He snorted. He reared, jerking the lead rope out of Jasmine's hand, and took off after the other ponies.

Jasmine took off after him, but Outlaw was fast.

"Outlaw!" Jasmine yelled, still running. "Don't run! You could hurt yourself."

Outlaw put his head down and ran as fast as he could.

"Please," Jasmine called. "I'll never mention the show again."

Outlaw stumbled and fell.

As Jasmine got to him, he was struggling to his feet.

"Are you okay?" she said.

His eyes were full of pain.

"Where does it hurt?" she said.

Outlaw nickered and looked down. He was holding his right hoof off the ground.

"It's my fault," Jasmine said. "I've been acting like a creep." Tears ran down her face. "Other ponies have normal owners. You have a nut."

Outlaw nudged her with his nose as if to tell her not to be so hard on herself.

She kissed her fingertips and put them on Outlaw's right ankle. This was a pretty silly thing to do, but when Jasmine was little and she hurt herself, her mother used to kiss the hurt place, and it always made Jasmine feel better.

Outlaw stared at her with his big brown eyes.

"Can you walk?" she asked. He took a tentative step. He winced, but he kept going.

The two of them struggled down the hill. As they neared the barn, Outlaw's limp got worse. Jasmine could tell that his ankle was hurting even more.

She led him into his stall. Gently she took off his bridle and saddle. "I'm going to get Judy Barker," she explained. "Judy will know what to do." Judy was Pine Hollow's horse veterinarian.

Outlaw dropped his head and poked his ankle with his nose as if he were trying to figure out what was wrong with it.

Jasmine ran into the house to call Judy.

Her father was on the phone. Jasmine touched his arm to let him know she needed to make a call. He held up a finger to show her he'd be done in a moment.

"You wouldn't believe such a big cough could come from such a little thing," Mr. James said. "It scares me."

Jasmine realized that Sophie, her baby sister, must be sick.

"She snuffles," Jasmine's father said. "But what's most worrisome is that cough. It's so deep."

Jasmine tugged his sleeve. "Is Sophie okay?"

Mr. James nodded reassuringly. "I'm talking to Dr. Santiago." He was the family pediatrician.

Everything is going wrong, Jasmine thought. Sophie is sick. Outlaw is injured.

She began to think of the pictures in her riding book. There was a whole chapter devoted to injuries of the foot. Outlaw's sore ankle might not be just a sore ankle. It could be a strained tendon. Or a torn tendon. Or it could be a curb, a strain of the ligament at the back of the leg.

Jasmine tried to make herself stop thinking these horrible thoughts. But all she could think of was the picture in the book of a pony with his legs in bandages. If a leg injury was really bad, Jasmine knew, sometimes a pony could never be ridden again.

"Dad!" Jasmine said. "It's an emergency."

"I've got to go," her father said into the phone.

As he hung up, Mr. James asked, "What's wrong?"

"Outlaw hurt his ankle," Jasmine said. "He can hardly walk."

Mr. James put his arm around her. "Let's go look. And then we can phone Judy Barker."

4 May's Great Idea

"My saddle is a disaster!" someone wailed.

May and Corey looked at each other and grinned. Excitement about the show was building. By Saturday everyone would be in a tizzy.

May and Corey were helping Judy Barker examine the Pine Hollow horses and ponies in preparation for the show.

"Nickel looks fine," said Judy Barker as she backed out of his stall. Corey, who was holding Judy's records, found Nickel's file and handed it to her. Judy made a few notes.

"The ponies can tell something's coming," Judy said. "By the end of the week they'll be as keyed up as the riders."

Judy handed the file back to Corey. "It's great to have an assistant who knows what to do," she said.

Corey flushed with pleasure. Lately she'd been thinking that she wanted to be a vet like her mother and Judy. Maybe someday she'd be examining ponies before a show, just like this.

The cellular phone in the pocket of Judy's blue blazer cheeped. It didn't sound like a regular phone. It sounded more like a bug.

Judy pulled out the phone and opened it. "Hello," she said. Her eyebrows shot up. "Jasmine." She looked at May and Corey because she knew the three of them were best friends.

May and Corey moved closer. What could be wrong?

"I'll be over as soon as I can," Judy said. She looked down the aisle of the barn. "I've got ten more horses to check. Then I'll be on my way."

May and Corey looked at each other.

Judy closed the phone. "Outlaw twisted his ankle," she said.

"We've got to go help Jasmine," May said. She looked around for her father. He was standing in the doorway of the office, talking to Mrs. Reg, Max's mother. May ran over to him and said, "Jasmine just telephoned Judy and told her that Outlaw's hurt. We have to go home right away."

"I just finished. Let's go," Mr. Grover said. He went to get his horse.

May ran to the stall where Macaroni was munching on the hay in his feed net. He had the dreamy look he got when he was settling down for a long snooze.

"Outlaw is hurt," May said.

Macaroni heard the worry in her voice. He shook his head and stood up straight. As she saddled him, May muttered, "I knew it. I knew something was going to go wrong."

When May led Macaroni out to the mounting block, Corey was there already. Mr. Grover arrived a few seconds later.

"I hope it's not serious," Corey said.

May nodded grimly.

Mr. Grover opened the gate to the pasture. Jasmine's barn seemed very far away.

"I wish we could gallop," May said.

"No way," Mr. Grover said. "The ground is mucky. It's dangerous."

When they got to the gate that led into Jasmine's yard, Jasmine ran out of the barn, her hair tangled, her face white.

"I wrecked everything," she said. "The Dream Team. Outlaw."

Corey jumped off Sam and tied him to the fence. She put her arms around Jasmine.

May got off Macaroni and tied him. She put her arms around both her friends. "Judy's on her way. She'll know what to do." May smoothed Jasmine's tangled hair. "You've got to be calm and collected when Judy comes."

Jasmine took a deep breath. "Poise, that's what I need," she said.

"Let's go see Outlaw," May said. The three girls ran into the barn.

Outlaw's head was down, and his eyes were clouded. Usually he looked saucy and rambunctious. Now he looked miserable.

"I hate myself," Jasmine groaned.

Out in the yard they heard the rattle of Judy Barker's pickup truck. They heard Mr. James's deep voice as he talked to her. Then Judy appeared in the doorway of the barn.

"Outlaw was running and he caught his foot," Jasmine said.

Judy put her hand on Jasmine's shoulder. "It's wet and muddy in the fields. These things happen."

Judy went into Outlaw's stall and talked to him softly. She ran her hand over his back and down his neck, giving him time to get used to her presence. "Which ankle is it?" she asked over her shoulder.

"The right front one," said Jasmine.

Gently Judy touched Outlaw's ankle. He nickered but didn't try to pull his foot away. She lifted his leg and moved his foot back and forth. She checked the inside of his hoof. Then she put his foot down. She straightened up and walked to the end of the stall. "He'll have to take it easy until the beginning of next week, but then he'll be fine. It's a mild sprain."

"You mean he'll be okay?" said Jasmine.

Judy Barker smiled at Jasmine. "You can wrap his ankle. But mainly he needs to rest. He's a strong, healthy pony. He'll be fine."

Jasmine burst into tears of relief.

Judy fished a packet of tissues out of her veterinarian's bag. She offered one to Jasmine. "It seems like I'm always needing these," she said gently. Jasmine figured this was Judy's way of saying that it was okay to cry.

"I know you'll take good care of him," said Judy with a smile.

"Will I!" Jasmine said.

As Judy drove away, Jasmine said, "What a morning. I'm a frazzled wreck."

"I know how to fix that," said May with a confident smile. "Knock knock."

A knock-knock joke! Sometimes, Jasmine thought, May can be pretty silly.

"Who's there?" asked Jasmine.

"Wanda," said May.

36

"Wanda . . . who?"

"Wanda come over and play?" said May.

"That's the worst knock-knock joke I ever heard," Corey said.

"I thought so myself," said May proudly.

Suddenly Jasmine felt a little better. At first she'd been disappointed that she couldn't ride in the show. Now she knew she could handle it.

"Now that I can't be in the show, I'll be your number one fan," she said. "I'll lead the cheers."

"Excuse me?" said May.

"I'll root you on to victory," Jasmine said.

"Not so fast," said May, crossing her arms.

"Outlaw has to rest. I can't ride," Jasmine said.

"You *are* going to ride," May said.

"Without a pony?" Jasmine asked.

Corey was dying of curiosity. "What's up?"

"I have a great idea," May said.

"Not another great idea," Jasmine groaned. "It's been a rough day. I can't take a great idea."

"Wait till you hear this one," May said. "We only have two ponies for three riders. But when did a little thing like that stop the Dream Team? We'll share ponies. You can ride Macaroni in the Equitation Class and Samurai in the Relay Race."

Jasmine knew how much May loved to ride in shows. "You'd do that for me? You'd give up riding in the Equitation Class?"

"I'm doing Macaroni a favor," May said. "You're a lot better at equitation than I am."

"Not!" said Jasmine.

"I want you to ride in the Relay Race," Corey said. "You'll be great."

Jasmine put her arms around her friends. "You two are the greatest. The Dream Team lives."

"And it's dreamier than ever," said May.

5 A Bad Hair Day

When Jasmine woke on Saturday, the morning of the horse show, she was excited. She got up and put on her best riding clothes. She looked at herself in the mirror and saw that she looked like a real rider, not a beginner. She sighed with relief.

But something was missing. She stared at herself, trying to figure out what it could be. Her new black riding jacket was sleek and unwrinkled. Her black riding hat was velvety. Her boots gleamed.

So what was missing? She scratched her head, trying to remember. It began to come back to her. Head. Hair.

She remembered. She and May and Corey had agreed to wear ponytails to show that they were members of the Pony Tail Dream Team.

Jasmine didn't usually wear a ponytail. Her hair was too flyaway for that. But she'd do anything for the Pony Tails. She went to the kitchen and got a rubber band. It was red and festive-looking. She thought it would be just right.

She took it upstairs and laid it on her dresser. Then she brushed her hair back. The top lay down nicely, but then the sides stuck out like crazy. She brushed the left side, and then the top and the right side stuck out. She brushed the right side, and the left side popped out.

"I hate my hair," she muttered.

She took both hands and pulled her hair back. She crammed all her hair into one hand and grabbed the red rubber band and twisted it around her ponytail once and then twice. It stung. Her hair wasn't used to being held so tight. She let go. Her ponytail stood out in all directions like a fan.

"I wish I were bald," she said.

But she wasn't bald, and she had to do something. She realized that her mother had hair just like hers. Her mother would know what to do. Jasmine went down the hall to her parents' room.

The door was closed, so Jasmine knocked.

"Come in," came her mother's voice.

Jasmine opened the door. Her mother was sitting in bed with Sophie in her arms. Her mom had dark circles under her eyes.

"Sophie was coughing so much we called the doctor during the night," Mrs. James said. "That's why we shut the door. We didn't want the noise to wake you."

From the slump of her mother's shoulders and the paleness of her face, Jasmine could tell that her mother hadn't gotten much sleep.

"You look wonderful in your riding clothes," said Mrs. James with a smile.

"I do?" said Jasmine. Obviously her mother was so tired that she couldn't see straight.

"What's wrong?" asked Mr. James. He was sitting on the edge of the bed, but he didn't look quite as tired as Mrs. James. He could tell that something was bothering Jasmine.

"It's my—" Jasmine began.

Sophie coughed. Her face turned red. Her eyes filled with tears.

"We're taking her to the hospital," Mrs. James said. "Dr. Santiago wants us there at ten."

The hospital! Jasmine panicked.

"It's just for tests," Mrs. James said. "Dr. Santiago can't do some tests at his office because he doesn't have all the equipment he needs."

How can going to the hospital not be serious? Jasmine wondered.

"Go downstairs and have some breakfast," Mrs. James said to Jasmine. "You're going to need lots of energy."

When Jasmine got to the kitchen, she propped her horse book against the sugar bowl and read it while she tried to eat. "Heels down," she read. "Hands up, knees in, back firm but not tense." She

43

raised a spoonful of cereal toward her mouth. It didn't look tasty at all. She put it back in the bowl.

"A light and easy carriage should be maintained at all times," she read. Her stomach began to hurt.

A few minutes later Mr. James came downstairs. "I'll drive you to Pine Hollow," he said. Then he took another look at her. "Are you okay?"

"I'm okay," Jasmine said. She pulled her riding hat over her horrible ponytail and headed for the door.

6 Dead Last

"And now May the Magnificent and her marvelous mount, the magical Macaroni," said May into an imaginary microphone. She and Corey had groomed and saddled Samurai and Macaroni. They had nothing left to do, so May was clowning around.

"Don't you ever get nervous?" asked Corey.

"I am nervous," May said. "This is what I do when I'm nervous. I act like a dope." May raised her arms like a rock star quieting a crowd. "And now Corey the Courageous on her standout steed, Samurai."

Corey couldn't resist. She doffed her riding hat as if she were bowing to a crowd.

"Your ponytail looks great," May said.

Corey had short, straight black hair, which made a terrific ponytail. "Let me see yours," Corey said.

May raised her hat. Usually May's hair was a tangled mess, but now it was neatly combed into a perfect ponytail.

"Is that you?" Corey said.

"I can't disgrace the Dream Team," May said. "I did the unthinkable. I asked Ellie to help me with my hair." Ellie was one of May's older sisters. She had few talents. But one of them was styling hair.

They put their hats back on their heads and fastened the chin straps.

"Too bad the Pony Tails don't have a theme song," May said. Her face lit up. "Hey, wait a minute. I feel a song coming on." To the tune of "Ta Ra Ra Boom De Ay" she sang, "We are the Pony Tails, we carry water pails, we keep our heels low, over the jumps we go."

"It's a hit," said Corey. "Kind of."

A sad, droopy thing appeared around

46

the corner of the barn. Corey took a look, and then another. It was Jasmine. She was wearing a velvety new hat, a spiffy new coat, and shiny black boots. But she looked miserable.

"Are you sick?" Corey said.

Jasmine shook her head.

"Is Outlaw worse?" asked May.

"It's Sophie," Jasmine said. "She looks awful. You should hear her cough. They're taking her to the hospital—"

"That's terrible!" May said.

"For tests," said Jasmine.

Corey let out a sigh of relief. "Dr. Santiago sends babies to the hospital for tests a lot. Babies are so tiny they need special equipment." She knew this because Dr. Santiago and her mother were friends.

"Really?" Jasmine said.

"Truly," Corey said.

Jasmine let out a sigh of relief.

"Okay," May said. "Down to business. It's time for the Dream Team to do a final check. Riders first."

The girls inspected each other's boots and clothes. Everything looked fine.

"Ponies next," May said.

47

The girls checked the ponies' hooves and coats and tacks. Everything was okay.

Over the loudspeaker came a voice: "Class number one. Showing and Sitting." In this class a pony stood still while his rider sat on him. Then the rider got off and stood next to the pony while the judges inspected his tack.

"Let's go," May said. She and Corey were participating in this class. May hugged Jasmine and went over to Macaroni's head to whisper a few last words to him. She mounted and rode into the ring. Corey hugged Jasmine, mounted Sam, and followed.

Jasmine leaned against the fence to watch them ride.

Samurai wasn't the world's most patient pony. There was a possibility he would start switching his tail and stamping his hooves, demonstrating that he thought Showing and Sitting was dumb. The judges wouldn't like that *at all*.

"Be good," Jasmine whispered to Samurai from the sidelines. "Be patient."

Samurai couldn't hear her because the

48

loudspeaker was blaring and the crowd was chattering, but it seemed as if he had. He stood with his head high, his eyes straight forward, and the white sword on his nose gleaming.

Macaroni stood still. Too still. May was trying to be extra-calm, so she wasn't bugging him at all. But Macaroni needed a little bugging. At the moment, he was so mellow that he looked as if he might go to sleep.

The judges gave first prize to Samurai and third to Macaroni. Last prize went to a boy called Jeff. It was clearly Jeff's first horse show. He looked as if he was about to faint from terror. Jasmine knew how he felt.

Next came the Pleasure Class. The point of the class was to see how much a pony enjoyed being ridden. May leaned over to Macaroni and whispered, "Please, Mac, be a little nervous. Don't mellow out on me."

The minute they started moving around the ring, Macaroni got into the spirit of things. He shook his yellow mane and lifted his feet high. May grinned with pleasure. This was Macaroni at his best. When he finished, the judges were looking at him with approval.

Samurai, on the other hand, had trouble with transitions. He switched from a walk to a trot with a bump, and from a trot to a canter with a lurch. He didn't do a terrible job, but he wasn't great. May came in first. Second prize went to a pony called Silver ridden by a girl named Lois, who gave Corey a superior smirk. Samurai came in third.

"Equitation," said the voice over the loudspeaker.

I'm not ready, Jasmine thought. She loved Macaroni, but she wasn't used to riding him. Riding Outlaw, Jasmine hardly had to signal. Riding Macaroni would be an experiment.

Poise, Jasmine thought. I must have poise. She felt like giggling and realized that this was part of being nervous.

May climbed off Macaroni and handed Jasmine the reins. "He's ready," she said. "He's looking forward to it."

Jasmine put her arms around Macaroni and said, "Thanks for letting me ride you. You're one great pony." He nuzzled her ear.

But when she got on his back, Macaroni turned to look at her as if he were puzzled.

"It's equitation," she said. "You love equitation."

Macaroni looked at May.

"Jasmine is fantastic at equitation," May said to him. "You're going to love her."

Not! thought Jasmine.

As they entered the ring, Macaroni looked back at May as if to ask her if she was sure.

Corey and Samurai were right behind them. Corey gave Jasmine a thumbs-up sign.

"Walk," said the voice over the loud-speaker.

Relax, Jasmine told herself, relax, relax.

She could feel tension in her stomach. It began to spread to her fingers and toes. Beneath her Macaroni was walking easily. But there was something wrong with his walk. It wasn't like Outlaw's walk. For Jasmine it was like wearing someone else's shoes.

"Trot," called the voice over the loudspeaker.

Jasmine pressed her knees together slightly—Macaroni was such an experienced pony he didn't need a big signal. Macaroni moved into a high-stepping trot. Jasmine knew it was a picture-book trot. Every element in it was perfect. But it was slower than Outlaw's trot. Jasmine found herself rising too soon, anticipating Macaroni by a fraction of a second. This was very dangerous, she knew. When a rider gets out of rhythm, her posting can get worse and worse until she's bouncing.

Slow down, she told herself. But then she was *too* slow. Beneath her she could feel Macaroni speed up and then slow down, struggling to get in tune with her. But keeping rhythm was her job, not his. It was a big relief when the voice over the loudspeaker said, "Canter."

She touched him behind the girth with her heel, and Macaroni moved effortlessly into his smooth, rocking canter. Jasmine enjoyed the slow, graceful motion.

That's it, she thought. We're almost done.

She saw something familiar out of the corner of her eye. She turned to look. It was her father. He looked pale. His hair was rumpled. Jasmine was sure something terrible had happened to Sophie. Without realizing it, she snapped her knees tight.

Macaroni thought it was a signal to gallop. He took off. Jasmine lurched forward. She lost her left stirrup and then her right. She slipped. She started to fall against Macaroni's neck. She dodged left to miss it and felt her bottom slide in the saddle. She could see the veins in Macaroni's neck. Dust rose into her eyes. She grabbed his mane and with a huge effort pulled herself upright as Macaroni galloped faster and faster.

"Canter, *please*," said the voice over the loudspeaker.

Jasmine knew she and Macaroni were in danger of spooking the other ponies.

But she couldn't slow Macaroni because he was as freaked as she was.

In the judges' box she could see Max looking at her with worry.

Something happened inside her brain. A small voice said, *Poise*.

She felt like laughing. With Macaroni running and the announcer telling her to slow down, how could she have poise?

She saw Max again, and all at once she felt as if she could do it. She knew Max had faith in her.

She looked down and realized that she was sawing at the reins, which only made Macaroni more frazzled. She loosened the reins and put a gentle hand on his withers. His stride shortened. Suddenly they were back in the easy rocking canter. Jasmine looked at Max, and his eyes were full of relief.

"Line up for judging," called the voice.

At least it was over, Jasmine thought. Her shirttail was out, her coat had popped a button, and her riding hat was halfway down her forehead. As she lined up with the other riders, she tried to put herself in order. She tucked in her shirt and straightened her coat. She un-snapped her chin strap and lifted her hat to straighten it.

Her ponytail bounced straight up. Jasmine could feel the hair stand on end. Everyone in the bleachers was staring at her. And then—worst of all—she looked at her father and saw that he was video-taping her.

"Judges, your decisions, please," said the voice over the loudspeaker.

Corey came in first. Jasmine came in fifth out of five.

7 The Pits of the Pits

"You held on," Mr. James said. "You got Macaroni back into a canter. You were great."

"If that's great," Jasmine said, "what's terrible?"

"You didn't panic," Mr. James said. "You kept your head."

"What head?" Jasmine said miserably. "By accident I gave Macaroni the signal to gallop. He was only following my dumb directions."

Mr. James put his arms around her. "It wasn't as bad as you think."

"How's Sophie?" Jasmine said, remembering that it was her father's pale face that had spooked her in the first place.

"She's much better," Mr. James said.

"At least something good happened," Jasmine said. "She's not going to stay in the hospital, is she?"

"She's sleeping at home," Mr. James said. "This afternoon I'm going to take care of her so your mom can come."

"Give Sophie a hug for me," said Jasmine.

"I'll give her two," her father said with a smile. "I'd better get home now. Good luck this afternoon."

As Mr. James left, May put her arm through Jasmine's. "Lets go have lunch on the PTSP." The horses and ponies had been stabled for the lunch break.

"I'm not very hungry," said Jasmine. She put her hand over her stomach. She didn't feel hungry at all. In fact, she felt definitely *un*hungry.

"I've got sandwiches," May said. Before anyone could say anything, May added, "My mother made them, not me. They're *normal* sandwiches."

58

"No banana-salami sandwiches?" asked Corey.

May shook her head.

"No pickles and date nut bread?" asked Corey.

"Sorry, not today," said May.

"Rats," said Corey with a grin. "Anyway, I've got special fruit shakes my mom made." Doc Tock was famous for her fabulous fruit shakes.

Jasmine realized that usually she would have brought some of her mother's great homemade cookies. But this wasn't a usual weekend. Her mother was at home with Sophie. And Jasmine was here, making a fool of herself.

As they walked up the hill, Jasmine said, "Have you ever heard of serendipity?"

"Is it a rock group?" asked May.

"It's a word for unexpected luck," Jasmine said. "My dad says that serendipity is when luck just happens." They climbed a few more steps. "What do you call the opposite of serendipity?"

"You mean like when catastrophe just happens?" asked Corey with a giggle.

"That's it," Jasmine said. "And that's what happened to me today."

"The pits," said May.

"This *is* the pits," Jasmine said. "The pits of the pits."

They got to the top of the hill and flopped down on the silvery grass that grew under the oak tree.

"At least I'm finished for the day," Jasmine said.

May crossed her arms. "Excuse me?"

"I can't ride anymore," Jasmine said.

"Why not?" May said.

"Because I've brought enough shame on the Dream Team for one day. I'm not going to bring more," Jasmine said. "You'll do better without me."

"Max says riders should never give up, no matter how terrible things get," Corey said. "He says the worse things get, the harder you should try."

"Did you ever see an ice-skater fall down?" asked May. "Like *splat*. Like *kaboom*. In front of millions of people."

Jasmine nodded.

"Or a gymnast fall off the bars," Corey said. "You know what they do?"

"They cry," Jasmine said.

"No," May said. "They get up and go on and finish the routine. Then they cry."

"Those are stars," Jasmine said. "I'm not exactly a star."

"You're Jasmine the Great," said May, "and don't you forget it."

"Soon to be on the cover of *Horrible Hair* magazine," said Jasmine, touching her ponytail.

"I can fix that," said Corey with a smile. She got up and went down to the stable and into Mrs. Reg's office. In a few minutes she came back with a pair of scissors and two rubber bands.

"I already went the rubber band route," groaned Jasmine.

"Wait and see," said Corey. She cut the red rubber band out of Jasmine's hair and then combed her hair gently until it was lying flat. She gathered the hair into a ponytail and put a rubber band around it. Somehow, Jasmine realized, when Corey did this, it didn't hurt. Corey braided the ponytail and fastened the bottom with the other rubber band.

61

Jasmine touched it. "It's not wild and crazy."

"It's neat and spiffy," May said.

Jasmine sighed. "Corey, you're not only good at horse grooming, you're good at people grooming," she said.

"Time for lunch," said May, who was always hungry.

There were peanut butter and strawberry jam sandwiches, and tuna salad and sprout sandwiches. These were two of Jasmine's favorites. But she wasn't hungry.

Corey and May polished off their sandwiches and fruit shakes. When they were done, the girls lay on their backs watching the slow movement of the oak tree.

"The Pony Tails are the greatest," said Jasmine.

"To think I lived all those years without being a Pony Tail," Corey said. "It's unbelievable." Corey had moved to Pine Hollow not long before.

From down the hill came the faint sound of the loudspeaker. "Riders assemble for the afternoon session."

May and Corey jumped up.

Jasmine sat up slowly. "Here goes."

As they walked down the hill, Jasmine saw her family's station wagon pull into the parking lot. Her mother got out, carrying the dreaded video camera.

Maybe someone will steal it, Jasmine thought. But Pine Hollow was a pretty safe place. The chances that anyone would steal the camera were slim. She considered hiring someone to steal it but realized she had other things to do.

The Grovers' station wagon, with a horse trailer behind it, pulled into the parking lot. Out of the station wagon stepped not just May's parents, but May's sisters, Dottie and Ellie, as well. May's sisters loved to tease. If Jasmine messed up this afternoon, as she surely would, she'd never hear the end of it.

The first event of the afternoon was the Pony Hunter Class. This class was judged for style. It didn't matter how fast riders rode around the course. It only mattered how well they did it. Corey and Samurai loved this event.

Sam trotted out, his head high. Jasmine could tell from the look on Corey's face that she wasn't aware of the crowd or of the judges. It was just her and Sam. With a slow, easy gait, Sam cantered toward the first jump. He rose smoothly. He landed without a bump. Corey's heels were down and her wrists were relaxed. From the happy look on her face Jasmine could tell that everything was perfect. Sam sailed through the rest of the jumps.

Then it was May and Macaroni's turn. Macaroni looked at the jumps and snorted, as if to say "No big deal."

He cleared the first two jumps with ease. He jumped the hedge without harming a leaf. Macaroni was doing a great job.

"Just one more, Mac," May said, and started to lean forward. But then she realized that she was doing the exact thing she'd resolved not to do. She was anticipating the jump. She eased back and took a deep breath. *Then* she leaned forward.

She was too late. Macaroni's left hind hoof clipped the rail. The rail trembled and fell.

First prize went to Sam and Corey,

with a special commendation for elegance. May and Macaroni came in third.

Then it was time for the Relay Race. May was captain of the Red Team. Originally, Corey was supposed to be on the Red Team, which would have made May's job a lot easier because Corey was an experienced relay rider. Now, with Corey off the team, the fourth spot was filled by Jeff, the new rider who looked as if he was going to faint from fear. May gave the team a pep talk, saying that though they might be underdogs, they had guts, so they were bound to have glory.

Lois, the snobby rider who had laughed at Corey in the Pleasure Class, said, "Jeff . . . glory. Somehow the two don't go together."

Naturally, this made Jeff look even more nervous.

"We're a team," May said. "All for one and one for all." She gave Lois a stern look. "Have you got that?"

The Relay Race was divided into three parts: the crop pass, the apple toss, and the egg and spoon race.

May started the crop pass with a cow-
boy yell. She and Macaroni dashed down
the ring to the spot where a red ribbon
was tied to the white fence. She touched
the crop to the ribbon. She rode back to
the other end of the ring and held out the
crop to Jeff.

He looked as if he wished he were on
Mars—anyplace but here. "Go, Jeff," said
May. Jeff reached for the crop. It wobbled
in his hand. Was he going to drop it?

He didn't. He held it so tightly that his
knuckles turned white. He and his pony,
Zoom, cantered briskly to the other end
of the ring.

"Zoom is zooming," said May to Jasmine with a grin. "I knew that kid could
do it." By the time Jeff got back, the Red
Team was only slightly behind the Blue
Team.

Next came Lois. She grabbed the crop
from Jeff's hand and sped forward. "Not
a good team player," said May to Jasmine. Lois cantered to the ribbon. Show-
ily she tapped the crop against it and said
something to her pony, Silver, who tore
back to the starting line. Disdainfully Lois

handed the crop to Jasmine. She seemed to be saying that Jasmine couldn't do half as well as she had.

"Let's show her," Jasmine said to Samurai. "Go for it." Sam put his head down and stretched his legs into a long, swift canter. (Galloping was forbidden in the Relay Race.) Jasmine headed Samurai into a loop so that she could reach out and touch the ribbon without stopping. When they got back to the finish line, the Red Team was two pony lengths ahead of the Blues. The judges awarded the Reds ten points and the Blues eight.

"Nice racing," May said to her team. "In the apple toss we're going to do even better."

Two of the judges came out of the judges' box. They stood close to May and the Blue Team rider and tossed them red apples.

May, who loved to play catch with her father, caught the apple in one hand and took off. She headed toward the three bales of hay at the far end of the ring. She kept her heels down and her knees tight. Mac, who was totally into the spirit of the

68

race, tore around the bales. By the time they got to the finish line, they were three lengths ahead.

May rode up to Jeff. She tossed the apple to him from two inches away.

The apple rolled out of his hand. Quick as a flash, Zoom took a bite out of it. The crowd roared with laughter. Under his riding hat, Jeff seemed to shrink.

A judge came over and carefully tossed another apple to Jeff. He caught it, but by this time the Blue Team was three lengths ahead. Bravely Jeff urged Zoom forward. Zoom took off.

Jeff rounded the three bales and headed for the finish line.

"Throw me the apple," Lois yelled. "I'm a great catcher."

Jeff looked at her with horror. He's probably a terrible thrower, Jasmine thought. Jeff rode up to the finish line and gave the apple a tiny little toss to Lois.

"You ruined everything," Lois said as she caught it. She and her pony sped around the bales. When Lois was ten feet from the finish line, she raised her arm and fired the apple at Jasmine.

69

Jasmine's stomach lurched. She wasn't a good catcher. She put up her hand and felt something hit it. She looked at her hand in astonishment. Somehow her fingers had closed around the apple.

"Go!" May yelled.

Samurai seemed to know it was up to him. He tore around the bales, his mane streaming in the wind. He and Jasmine passed the Blue rider. By the time they got to the finish line, they were a length ahead.

The Red Team had finished ahead of the Blue, but there was a three-point penalty for dropping the apple. The judges awarded the Red Team seven points and the Blue Team nine. Going into the last stage of the race, the teams were tied 17 to 17.

In the egg and spoon race riders had to balance an egg while they followed a twisting, turning course. It was by far the toughest part of the race.

"This is going to be a million laughs," said Lois, looking at Jeff.

"It's going to be the Red Team's finest hour," said May. "Wait and see."

May was first. She let out a whoop, and she and Macaroni took off. Macaroni cantered around the orange marker and made a perfect curve toward the trash can. He ran around the trash can twice, the way he was supposed to, and headed for the pile of hay bales. He passed them on the right and headed for home. By the time he and May got to the handoff, the Red Team was two lengths ahead.

Carefully May rolled the egg into Jeff's spoon.

"You'll be great," May said.

"Don't drop it," Lois said.

That did it. Jeff held the spoon so stiffly that the egg skittered back and forth. Looking at the wobbling egg with horror, Jeff slowed Zoom to a crawl. By the time he got to the handoff, the Reds were three lengths behind.

"Watch this," said Lois as Jeff rolled the egg into her spoon. "You're going to see some real riding." She kicked Silver. The pony took off like a rocket. Lois leaned forward, balancing the egg.

"Ho boy," May said. "She's going to drop it."

As Lois made the turn around the orange marker, her face filled with fear. She was going so fast, she'd lost control of her pony. Silver's head was down, his hoofs flying. Lois wasn't even trying to steer him; she was too busy balancing the egg. As Silver careened around the trash basket, the egg rolled. As they zoomed past the hay bales, it bounced.

As Lois came closer and closer, Jasmine held out her spoon.

The egg flew off Lois's spoon.

8 Splat!

"Catch that egg," yelled May.

Jasmine stretched and leaned and caught the egg. The spoon and egg were down by her boot. It would be impossible to get them up. But Sam seemed to understand. He ran so gently, his feet seemed to barely touch the ground. Jasmine pulled the spoon up and up. It was at waist level now. She heaved a sigh of relief.

"Go, Red!" came a piercing shriek. Sam jumped, rattled by the noise. Jasmine knew that voice. It was Lois. She was trying to spook Samurai. Thanks, Lois, Jasmine thought.

"We're going to turn now," she said to Samurai. "Turn gently. Turn . . ."

Samurai floated around the orange marker.

"You are the greatest," Jasmine said.

It was time to circle the trash can. "Easy," she said. Samurai ran gently right. The egg wobbled. Jasmine rose high in her stirrups and crouched like a jockey. Her form was terrible. But she had to hold on to that egg.

The Blue rider was slightly ahead. Jasmine pressed her knees to Samurai's sides, urging him to go faster. They caught up to the Blue rider as they rounded the bales and headed for the finish line.

"Go, Sam," she said.

Sam gave it all he had. The egg started to roll off the spoon. It trembled on the edge. Jasmine extended her arm until she was riding with it held straight out.

The finish line was straight ahead. "Almost there," she yelled. She held the spoon out in front of her because the first egg to cross the line was the winner. One step, two steps. They were almost there.

74

Jasmine was about to make a yell of victory, when . . .

The egg rolled off the spoon and went *splat!* on the finish line.

The Blue Team had won.

Jasmine sat staring down at the smashed egg. It was so small—it was nothing. While she was carrying it, the egg had seemed very big. For a second she was angry at the egg. What was its problem? Why hadn't it hung on for one second more?

Members of the Blue Team were yelling and cheering. In the stands their families were jumping and hugging each other. For a second Jasmine hated the Blue Team.

And then she hated herself. If it hadn't been for her, the Red Team would have been cheering now. And Jeff wouldn't have been crying. He had gotten off his pony and he was wiping his eyes. "It's my fault," he said. "I dropped the apple. I lost the race for everyone."

Jasmine realized that, more than anything, she wanted to make Jeff feel better.

"Hey!" she said. "Who dropped the

75

egg?" She jumped off Samurai and gave his reins to Corey. "I dropped it," Jasmine said. "And don't you forget it."

Jeff looked at her in wonder.

Jasmine put her hand on his shoulder. "The Red Team has pluck, and spirit, and determination, *and* butterfingers."

Jeff gave a grin that was halfway between laughter and tears.

"I bet this was your first show," Jasmine said. Jeff nodded. "Mine, too," Jasmine said. "I've been a nervous wreck for a week."

Jeff looked astonished that someone else could have had the same problem he had.

"I was sure everyone would laugh when I rode into the ring," Jasmine said. "I was sure I'd make a fool of myself. But that didn't happen at all. I didn't make a fool of myself. I made a *complete creep* of myself."

Jeff giggled.

Over Jeff's shoulder Jasmine saw Max. He had heard practically the whole conversation. Jasmine thought, Now Max is really going to think I'm a meatball. But she noticed that Max's blue eyes were shining.

"Time for riders to assess their goals," announced the voice over the loudspeaker.

"Goals?" said Jasmine, as her stomach fell to her feet. "Can't we just forget about them?"

"That's how they decide Best in Show," May said. "They see if riders have met their goals."

Max walked toward them with a handful of white envelopes. Never had envelopes looked so big or so scary to Jasmine.

Max turned to May. "You first," he said. He handed May her envelopes, one for each of the classes she'd ridden in. May opened the Sitting and Showing envelope and read her goal. " 'In the first two classes I want to be calm,' " she read. " 'Sometimes I get so excited I make Macaroni nervous.' " She shook her head. "I certainly didn't make him nervous today. He practically fell asleep."

"You let him be too relaxed," Max said. "But you're on the right track."

May opened the envelope for the Pony Hunter Class. "My goal was to not rush Macaroni," she said. "I started rushing him, but then I stopped. So I confused him, and we messed up the jump."

"At least you were trying," Max said. "That's why it's important to write down goals—so you can focus on what needs improvement."

May nodded. In her next show, she knew she'd do better.

May opened her last envelope. It was for the Relay Race. "My goal was to get the riders excited without making them nervous." She looked at Jeff, who was still jumpy and pale. "I don't seem to have succeeded."

Max cleared his throat and looked at Lois. May knew that Max never criticized Pine Hollow riders in front of other riders, but she had the feeling that he was sorely tempted at the moment. Max looked at her, his eyes shining. "There are some things you can't control," he said. "You did an excellent job."

May glowed.

"Corey, what about you?" Max said.

She opened her first envelope, the one for Showing and Sitting. "My goal was help Samurai stay interested," she said.

Max grinned. "You did a good job. He didn't goof off."

"In the Pony Hunter Class I wanted to keep my heels down and my wrists relaxed," Corey said.

"You did a fine job," Max said. He turned to Jasmine.

"It was my first show," Jasmine said. "I'm sorry. I'm sorry for everything."

"Read your goals," said Max.

"In Equitation my goal was to have poise." She laughed miserably. "That's a joke."

"You didn't fall off Macaroni," Max said. "You finished the event."

"Big deal," Jasmine muttered. Figuring she might as well get it over with, she opened the last envelope and read her goal for the Relay Race. She felt her face turn pink. " 'My goal for the Relay Race is to not drop the egg.' "

Into Jasmine's mind flashed a picture of the egg splattering on the finish line.

"You kept your cool under difficult circumstances. That's what horse shows are about." Max patted her shoulder. "And when it did drop, you were at the finish line in first place. After all it didn't splatter. Not bad." Max moved on to the other riders with a twinkle in his eye.

"You should feel really good," May said to Jasmine. "Max was impressed."

"Yeah, right," Jasmine said.

The Pony Tails waited nervously while Max talked to the other judges.

"Riders, assemble in the ring on your mounts," said the voice over the loudspeaker.

Jasmine straightened her hat and checked the buttons on her coat. Only then did she remember that she had no pony to ride. She looked at Max, who seemed to know exactly what she was thinking.

"Go on foot," he said. "Stand in the center near the judges."

As Jasmine walked into the ring, she felt silly. There were kids on ponies and horses, and then there were the judges, and then there was Jasmine. She must look as if she'd wandered into the ring by accident.

Jasmine realized that Max was watching her. She put her shoulders back and her head up and marched into the ring. She felt shy about standing near the judges. But Max motioned to her to come and stand near him.

The rows of ponies and horses were impressive. The kids on them were sitting straight. The loudspeaker was playing march music. The crowd was standing. Jasmine spotted her mother down at the front, camera raised, videotaping everything.

The music stopped. Not a single horse or pony fooled around. They seemed to understand the seriousness of the moment.

The head judge, a woman in a red jacket, took the microphone and said, "We will now announce Best in Show for the Pony Division." Her voice sounded scratchy and far away. "Corey Takamura on Samurai."

Jasmine whooped with joy. This was

the greatest. For a second she felt she should have been more dignified, but then she realized that the other riders were yelling and clapping, too.

The judge walked over to Corey and gave her the ribbon. Corey sat very still while the crowd applauded.

"Second Best in Show in the Pony Division, May Grover on Macaroni," said the judge.

Jasmine felt relieved. She had been afraid that by wrecking the Relay Race she had wrecked things for May. But the judges had seen how well May led her team. They understood that it wasn't her fault when Jasmine dropped the egg.

May touched her hat and grinned. Since May was popular not just with the riders but with their parents, there was lots of applause. Even May's sisters were applauding. Probably, Jasmine thought, they were applauding May's ponytail.

Then came the awards for the Horse Division. Carole Hanson came in first. Stevie Lake came in second. And Lisa Atwood came in third. Jasmine wasn't surprised. Carole, Stevie, and Lisa were members of The Saddle Club. The Pony Tails dreamed of being half as good as they were.

Jasmine thought that maybe, someday, she'd win a prize. But that day was far off.

Max stepped up to the microphone. "Finally," he said, "I want to announce the winner of the Max Award. This award is named after my grandfather, Max Regnery the First, the founder of Pine Hollow Stables. The Max Award is for the rider who has the most courage. Or, in the words of the award . . ." Max read the inscription: " 'the rider who has the most heart.' "

Max looked up. "In my opinion, and the opinion of the judges, there is only one candidate for this award. One rider suffered a loss but participated anyway. One rider was able to put her own feelings aside and comfort another."

Jasmine thought, That must be some rider. She looked around, trying to figure out who it was.

"Jasmine James," Max said.

There was an eruption of noise. Thunderstruck, Jasmine stared at the cheering, smiling people. She saw her mother waving the camera in the air and jumping up and down. Most of all, she saw Max's warm blue eyes.

She walked forward, feeling a little wobbly. What if I trip? she thought. That would be the worst thing on earth. But then she thought, I've done every other silly thing on earth, so tripping wouldn't be that big a deal.

She grinned. She relaxed.

Max gave her the award. It was a brass plaque attached to a piece of wood. He raised her hand so that she was holding it high in the air and everyone could see it.

May and Corey were practically dancing on their ponies. With all the cheering and the shouting, Jasmine couldn't hear what they were saying, but she didn't have to. She knew they were saying that the Dream Team was number one.

Jasmine realized they were right. The Dream Team had taken the top three prizes in the show.

9 Peace and Quiet?

"You've got heart," Mrs. James said proudly as they drove home in the family station wagon.

"Heartburn is more like it," Jasmine said. She hadn't eaten any breakfast or lunch, so the minute she got in the station wagon she had eaten four cookies, plus a brownie. Then she had drunk a container of orange juice, and now she felt . . . dreadful.

"Thank heavens I caught the whole thing on tape," Mrs. James said.

Jasmine shuddered, remembering how she'd nearly fallen off Macaroni in the morning, and how her ponytail had stood on end, and how she'd dropped the egg on the finish line. But then she thought it was nice that her mother had taped her getting the award. And without the bad stuff, the good stuff didn't make sense.

"*Erp,*" Jasmine said.

"What's that, dear?" her mother said.

"A burp," Jasmine said.

"Is there something wrong with the cookies?" Mrs. James asked worriedly.

"Mom, they were great," Jasmine said. "It's just that I ate too many."

The minute they had parked in the Jameses' garage, Jasmine jumped out of the car and ran to the stable. Outlaw was half asleep.

"You'll never believe what I won," Jasmine said to him. "Look at this." She held out the award.

Outlaw woke up. He put his nose next to the award and sniffed it. But when he realized it wasn't something to eat, he yawned.

"It's the first of many," said May. She and Corey were leaning over the stall door, grinning. The Grovers had driven them and their ponies back from Pine Hollow.

"You're going to need a trophy room," said Corey.

"Not right this minute," Jasmine said. "I mean, it would have to be a really small trophy room. Like about six inches tall."

"Just wait," Corey said.

"So, admit it, your first horse show wasn't so bad," May said.

"Bad? It was the worst, the most terrifying, the most horrible experience of my life," Jasmine said. She sighed. "And the best because the three of us were together."

"Do you think Outlaw feels left out?" Corey asked. "He was the only one who wasn't there."

Jasmine looked at Outlaw, who was yawning again. "He seems to be handling it pretty well," she said.

Just to make sure, the three girls gave Outlaw a super-special Pony Tail grooming, and then they did the same for Macaroni and Samurai. Afterward they went to Jasmine's house to check the cookie jar.

Sure enough, it was crammed with peanut butter cookies. The Pony Tails filled a plate with cookies and poured themselves glasses of cold milk. They carried them upstairs to Jasmine's room.

"Back to normal," said Jasmine, flopping down on the bed. "I could use some peace and quiet."

"Peace and quiet? No way," said May. "My Pony Tail instincts tell me there's a new adventure coming on."

JASMINE'S TIPS ON DRESSING FOR A HORSE SHOW

There are two things you've really got to know before you enter a horse show. The first is absolutely everything there is to know about horses, and the second is absolutely everything there is to know about riders. Well, maybe that's a slight exaggeration, but if you do know all those things, it'll definitely be helpful.

That's the way Max put it to us. I know he was joking, but it was a useful joke because there are always two sides to riding—the pony side and the rider side. Everybody knows that the pony has to be perfectly groomed before he can enter a show, so it's only logical that the rider has to be groomed, too. And there's a lot more to that than taking a bath and brushing your hair.

I love dressing up; I've always loved it. I love dressing my dolls, and I've had fun making costumes and special tack for my model horses. So it's no wonder I had fun dressing up for my horse show. Max told us at Horse Wise that there's a reason for everything we wear when we ride, and the reasons are always *comfort, safety,* and *tradition.* Personally, I think the *tradition* part was stuck in there to be the answer when *comfort* and *safety* don't apply, but that's okay. Tradition is fun.

You start with clean, comfortable underwear and socks. If you're going to look at ease while you're in the saddle, you'd better not have anything that itches, scratches, or bunches up underneath—anywhere, if you know what I mean.

Next come the pants. All riding pants should be snug so they won't wrinkle. That's not for looks, though. That's for comfort. In fact, it's so important for riding pants to be smooth that you'll notice there's no seam inside where your legs grip your pony. When I ride, I wear jodhpurs and short black boots called jodhpur boots. I also wear garters and pants clips so the jodhpurs won't wrinkle and rub at my knees. When I grow bigger, I'll wear breeches and high boots that come up to my knees. For now, my feet and I are growing at such a rapid rate that it doesn't make sense to buy tall, expensive boots. Jodhpurs come in a lot of different colors, but for a formal show, they should be white, yellow, or tan. That's because of tradition. Mine are tan. I like that because they're less likely to show a smudge of dirt than white or yellow ones. That's for common sense.

Then comes a shirt. For a show, you have to wear a long-sleeved white cotton shirt. It's a special shirt with a neckband collar so you can also wear a stock. A

stock is a white tie, a little bit like an as-
cot. It matches the shirt, and it's held in
place with a gold safety pin through the
knot. Most of the reason for the shirt is
tradition.

Another thing that's traditional is the
riding coat. That's the jacket that goes
over the shirt. For a show, it has to be a
solid color—black, navy blue, or dark
gray. You've probably seen people wearing bright red jackets, but those aren't for
shows. Those are for hunting. If it's really,
really hot outside, sometimes the judges
will say that young riders don't have to
wear jackets, but you're going to have to
have one most of the time.

You can wear gloves if you want to. I
like to wear them sometimes. If it's cold
outside, they keep my hands warm, but
that's not really what they're for. They
help you grip the reins securely, so
they're for safety.

Once the rest of me is ready, I work on
my head. First of all, I have to do my hair.
The last thing a rider wants is to have her
hair fall in her face or get in the way. A

girl's hair can be braided, put in a ponytail, or made into a bun. After that, it goes in a hairnet. That makes me feel like a cafeteria lady, but the advantage riders have over cafeteria ladies is that we get to wear riding hats, and they cover everything. Thankfully, Max didn't make us wear nets at the Pine Hollow Show!

A riding hat is the biggest single safety item any rider wears. It has to be a black velvet, hard hunt cap that's ASTM/SEI certified. Those initials stand for American Society for Testing and Materials/ Safety Equipment Institute (I had to look that up). It's easy to remember that riding is fun, but it's important to remember that it can be dangerous. A good hat that fits snugly and is securely fastened under your chin is the first step in safe riding.

That's all the stuff you should wear, but there are a couple of things you can't wear. Don't bother with any jewelry, barrettes, or ribbons. Forget about dangles, bangles, rings, and pins. The only pieces of jewelry you're allowed to wear are your stock pin and a Pony Club pin (on your hat or collar). This is no time to wear perfume or cologne, either. It can annoy other riders, and it may irritate your pony.

And then there's one thing you should always wear, for safety, comfort, *and* tradition—your smile.

Good luck!

About the Author

Bonnie Bryant was born and raised in New York City, and she still lives there today. She spends her summers in a house on a lake in Massachusetts.

Ms. Bryant began writing about girls and horses when she started The Saddle Club series in 1987. So far there are more than sixty books in that series. Much as she likes telling the stories about Stevie, Carole, and Lisa, she decided that the younger riders at Pine Hollow Stables, especially May Grover, have stories of their own. That's how Pony Tails was born.

Ms. Bryant rides horses when she has time away from her computer, but she doesn't have a horse of her own. She likes to ride different horses, enjoying a variety of riding experiences. She thinks most of her readers are much better riders than she is!

*Don't miss the next exciting Pony Tails
adventure from Bonnie Bryant . . .*

MAY'S RUNAWAY RIDE
Pony Tails #14

May Grover is having one of those days.
Everyone is mad at her. First, she woke
up Jasmine's little sister. Then, she broke
the heel on one of her mother's favorite
shoes. Finally, she let a puppy out of his
pen, and Doc Tock had to chase him all
over the yard. May didn't mean to do
anything wrong, but she couldn't do anything right. When she goes riding with
her friend Joey Dutton and his father,
May is determined not to make any more
mistakes—but everything still goes
wrong! Now May's family and friends
think she has run away from home.